Hello Kitty® Everywhere!

PHOTOGRAPHS AND HAIKU

Concept and Photographs by
Jennifer Butefish and Maria Fernanda Soares

Text by Kate T. Williamson

HARRY N. ABRAMS, INC., PUBLISHERS

Departing To	Time	Remarks
New York Kennedy	7 00a	On Time
New York Kennedy	8 00a	On Time
New York LaGuardia	6 45a	On Time
Newark		On Time
Newark		Time
Orlando		Time
San Diego		Boa
San Diego		me
San Diego		me
San Diego		
San Diego		
San Diego		Time
San Jose		

Wednesday

INTRODUCTION

Like girls everywhere, Hello Kitty loves to travel.
Inspired by the great haiku master Bashō, Hello Kitty
has embarked on her own journey of exploration,
reflection, and making new friends.

From Hollywood to Paris, Kyoto to Kenya, Hello
Kitty's adventures take her to the far reaches of the
world and beyond. With each new experience, she
pauses to record her impressions in haiku form, using
three lines to capture one moment.

You'll be surprised at the many places she visits! And
remember, no matter where her travels may lead her,
there is one place where Hello Kitty will always be...
in your heart!

I'M A RISING STAR!
DO I HAVE TO CHANGE MY NAME?
YOUR AUTOGRAPH, PLEASE.

A FRIEND TO ALL BIRDS,
I STAND PROUDLY WITH THE CLOUDS—
THE RED, WHITE, AND CUTE!

PARLEZ-VOUS FRANÇAIS?
PLEASE DIRECT US TO THE SHOPS—
WE SEEK PINK BERETS.

DRIFTING TOWARD THE MOON,
I FLOAT IN A SEA OF STARS
AND TWINKLE WITH THEM.

DON'T FEAR, LITTLE WORLD!
FLYING THROUGH THE FLUFFY CLOUDS,
WE ARE HERE TO HELP!

VEIL OF FRAGILE LACE
A CHERRY TREE IN BLOSSOM—
MY HAPPIEST DAY!

SOARING HIGH ABOVE,
I SEE THE WORLD MORE CLEARLY.
BEST BEHAVIOR, PLEASE!

PINK BIRD DESCENDING.
CONTROL TOWER TO KITTY:
PERMISSION TO LAND.

SEAGULLS MAY SWOOP LOW,
BUT I ONLY HEAR THE WIND.
KITTY IN MOTION!

STANDING AT THE BAR,
I GAZE AT MY REFLECTION
AND FORGET TO DANCE.

THE FLAMES KEEP ME WARM,
LIKE A COZY WINTER'S FIRE.
I HAVE NO WORRIES.

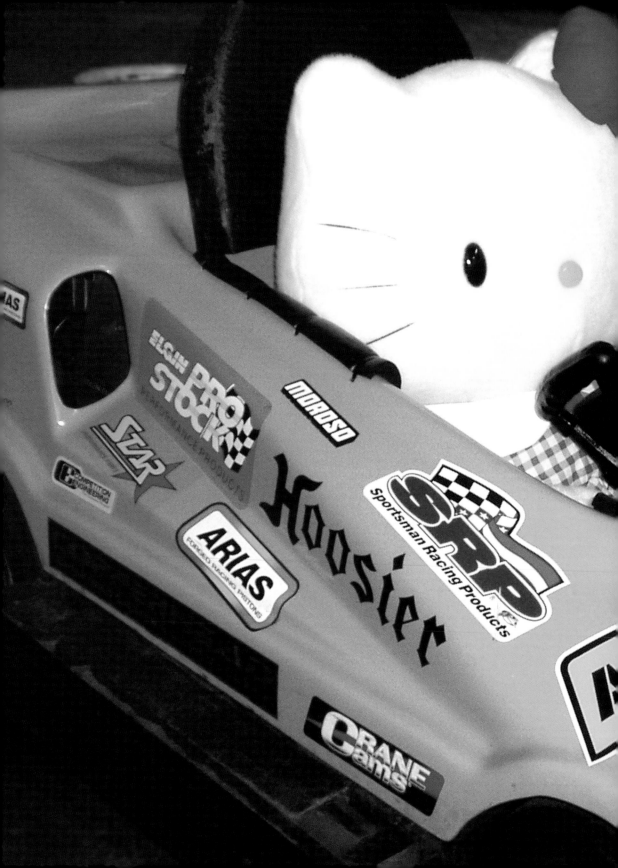

SCENT OF BURNT RUBBER,
PINK IS MY LUCKY COLOR—
VICTORY IS MINE.

SPRAY OF BLUE OCEAN,
I NEGLECT TO TRIM THE SAILS.
LET'S NOT CAPSIZE, PLEASE!

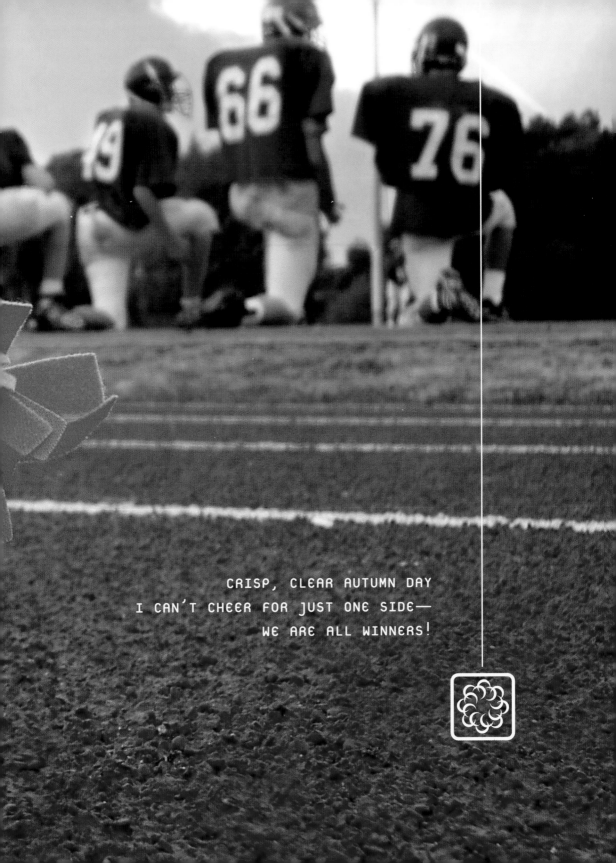

CRISP, CLEAR AUTUMN DAY
I CAN'T CHEER FOR JUST ONE SIDE—
WE ARE ALL WINNERS!

IN THE BLUE HALF-LIGHT
SCALES SHIMMER LIKE A RAINBOW.
MY WHISKERS ARE WET!

FIELD OF COLD COLORS
JUST ONE SHADE WILL MATCH MY DRESS—
I CHOOSE STRAWBERRY!

A WARM SUMMER WIND
KEEPS MY FRIEND VERY BUSY—
I ENJOY THE VIEW.

PEEKING THROUGH THE SOIL,
THE FLOWERS SHYLY EMERGE.
I AM THEIR FIRST FRIEND.

FROM MY ROCKY PERCH,
I SPY ONE PERFECT SPIDER—
HE SMILES BACK AT ME.

QUIET MOON FLOWER
HIDDEN ON THE FOREST FLOOR—
I BLOSSOM AT NIGHT.

DRESSED IN POLKA DOTS,
I FLY AMONG THE FLOWERS
AND PAUSE TO SPREAD LOVE.

SHIMMERING SNOWFLAKES
FLUTTER SOFTLY TO MY FACE
AND WAIT FOR SPRINGTIME.

SUDDEN SUMMER RAIN
AND WHERE IS MY UMBRELLA?
LOVE IS WATERPROOF.

HOT PINK AFTERNOON!
ALTHOUGH THE WATER BECKONS,
I'LL WORK ON MY TAN.

DANCING IN THE LIGHT,
THE WATER WHISPERS TO ME—
I BOB PEACEFULLY.

IN BETWEEN THE WAVES
COMES THE SOUND OF A SEASHELL—
I'M CARRIED TO SHORE.

GOING FOR A WALK—
MY FAVORITE TIME OF DAY.
WE BOTH MAKE NEW FRIENDS!

CIRCUS ELEPHANT,
LET ME HELP YOU WORK TODAY!
ALL PEANUTS ARE YOURS.

AS THE SPRING SUN SETS,
WE STOP TO COUNT THE RIPPLES—
A MAGICAL DAY.

COOL WATER FALLING
AMID THE MOSS-COVERED TREES—
I SIT HYPNOTIZED.

ENTRANCED BY THE KOI,
I DID NOT HEAR YOU APPROACH—
WON'T YOU WALK WITH ME?

WITH A SPLASH WE LEAP
AND PLUNGE BENEATH THE SURFACE!
OOPS—I LOST MY BOW!

I MAY LOOK SCARY,
BUT IT'S WHAT'S INSIDE THAT COUNTS—
LOVELY TO MEET YOU!

WIND WHISTLING SIDEWAYS,
I LISTEN TO THE CONCERT
AND HOLD ON TIGHTLY.

I PACE BACK AND FORTH,
BUT MY EYES ARE TRAINED ON YOU—
THIS KITTY IS WILD!

SILENTLY STALKING
WHEN IS THE MOMENT TO POUNCE?
I AM SO HUNGRY!

WITH HIS NECK OUTSTRETCHED,
MY FRIEND HELPS ME NAVIGATE—
I FEEL VERY SHORT.

FINISHED WITH MY CHORES,
I PRACTICE WITH MY LASSO.
LOOK OUT! A STAMPEDE!

AT ONE WITH MY HORSE—
IN ADDITION TO JUMPING,
WE BOTH ENJOY SWEETS.

WAITING QUIETLY
IN MY PUMPKIN HIDEAWAY—
SURPRISE, HERE I AM!

THE ORANGES AND I
SHARE A DELICATE SWEETNESS—
OUCH! NO SQUEEZING PLEASE!

CRAZY MONKEY GIRL
SWINGING NIMBLY THROUGH THE TREES—
GOING BANANAS!

THE WAVES LAP GENTLY
AS THE SALTY AIR GROWS COOL—
THANK YOU FOR TODAY!

THE SUN SAYS GOOD-BYE—
IN THE FADING AFTERGLOW,
I BEGIN MY DANCE.

CARRIED BY MY DREAMS,
I TRAVEL WITHOUT FLYING—
MORNING COMES TOO SOON.

Production Manager: Jonathan Lopes
Design and illustrations by Celina Carvalho

Concept and photographs by Jennifer Butefish and Maria Fernanda Soares
Text by Kate T. Williamson

Library of Congress Cataloging-in-Publication data has been applied for.

ISBN: 0-8109-4938-5

Printed and bound in China
10 9 8 7 6 5 4 3 2 1

Harry N. Abrams, Inc.
100 Fifth Avenue
New York, NY 10011
www.abramsbooks.com

Abrams is a subsidiary of

LA MARTINIÈRE
G R O U P E

SIL-3456